DREAMWORKS

Trolls
WORLD TOUR

♪ Rockin' Rainbow ♪

By Lauren Clauss

A GOLDEN BOOK • NEW YORK

ISBN 978-0-593-12233-4
rhcbooks.com
PENCIL MANUFACTURED IN CHINA
Book printed in the United States of America
10 9 8 7 6 5 4 3

This is Poppy.

Poppy is Queen of the Pop Trolls!

This is Branch.

Branch loves Poppy, but he doesn't know how to tell her.

Meet the Pop Trolls. They love pop music!

How many words can you make out of
POP TROLLS?

_____   _____

_____   _____

_____   _____

_____   _____

_____   _____

_____   _____

_____   _____

_____   _____

_____   _____

POSSIBLE ANSWERS: Loop, lost, lot, pot, roll, stoop, stop, toll, and top.

**This is Biggie. His favorite buddy is Mr. Dinkles.
They go everywhere together!**

Here is Cooper. He's a unique Troll.

This is Fuzzbert. He is an especially hairy Troll!

Pop Trolls have lots of fun!

This is Guy Diamond. He's covered in glitter!

What is the name of Guy Diamond's son? To find out, follow the lines and write each letter in the correct box.

N Y I T M O A D D I N

Tiny Diamond is a Hip-Hop Troll!

King Peppy is Poppy's father, and he is King of the Pop Trolls. He has a scroll that tells about all the different types of music!

Find the different kinds of music in the puzzle!
Look up, down, forward, backward, and diagonally.

POP • ROCK • COUNTRY WESTERN
FUNK • CLASSICAL • TECHNO

```
Z P A O T E S C R N P Q F G
B M S G D E R P L W L A Z V
D J I V S Y C Z W M O R A I
Y G K D A S B H X I F U N K
X U Z C H J E C N A I M L B
N P N I O O T R E Q E C H X
A O Y B R R N Q H L X I H Y
K P L J C Z H O G E B Y D L
T Z H I L A C I S S A L C H
I B P G J C P H Q R Z E Y D
C O U N T R Y W E S T E R N
```

Musical instruments are used to make music.
Unscramble these words to see the names of a few of them.
Write the words on the lines.

M R D S U

_____

T U F L E

_____

I U G A R T

_____

N O O C M E R P I H

_____

S B S A

_____

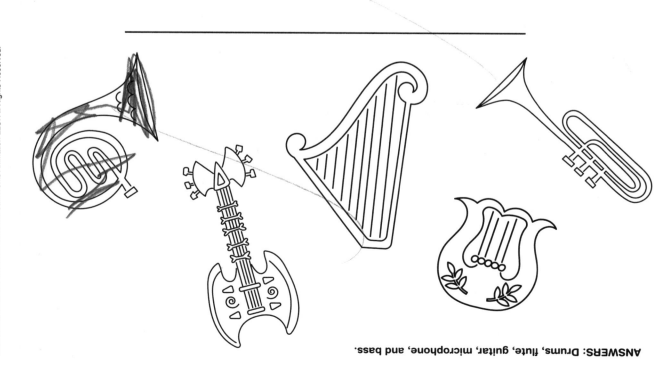

ANSWERS: Drums, flute, guitar, microphone, and bass.

Cooper sees on King Peppy's scroll that there are other Trolls who look like him!

Help Cooper get to Vibe City!

START

FINISH

ANSWER:

Cooper is a Funk Troll!
In Vibe City, he meets his brother, Prince D.

Cooper's parents are King Quincy and Queen Essence.
Cooper is a prince!

Poppy and Branch travel to meet other kinds of Trolls. Follow the letters in the word TROLL to find your way to their first stop: Symphonyville!

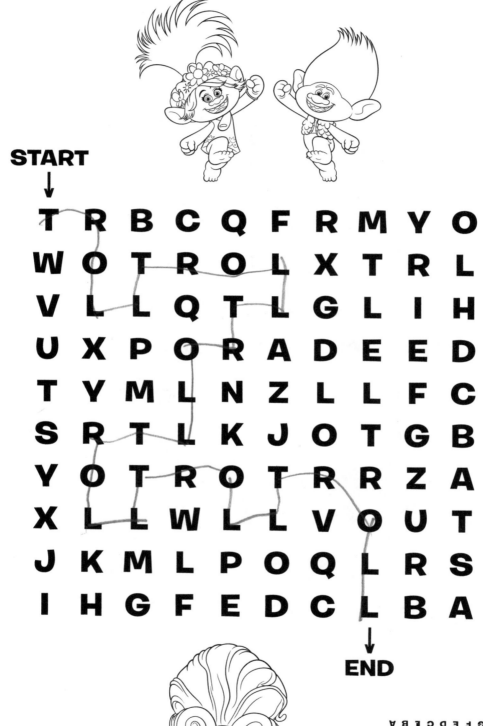

START

```
T  R  B  C  Q  F  R  M  Y  O
W  O  T  R  O  L  X  T  R  L
V  L  L  Q  T  L  G  L  I  H
U  X  P  O  R  A  D  E  E  D
T  Y  M  L  N  Z  L  L  F  C
S  R  T  L  K  J  O  T  G  B
Y  O  T  R  O  T  R  R  Z  A
X  L  L  W  L  L  V  O  U  T
J  K  M  L  P  O  Q  L  R  S
I  H  G  F  E  D  C  L  B  A
```

END

Meet Pennywhistle. She may be tiny, but she always makes her voice heard among the other instruments in town!

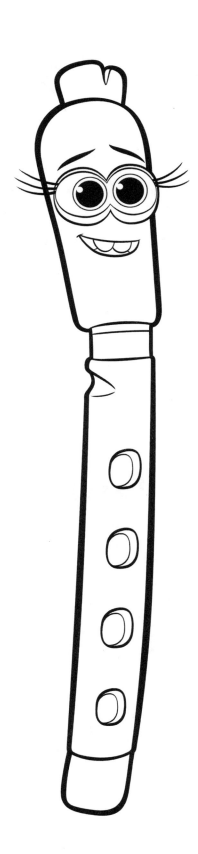

**Trollzart lives in Symphonyville.
He is the leader of the Classical Trolls.**

What is Trollzart's role in the orchestra? To find out, replace each letter with the one that comes before it in the alphabet. Write the letters on the blanks.

D P O E V D U P S

_ _ _ _ _ _ _ _ _

ANSWER: Conductor.

Which Trolls live underwater? To find out, start at the arrow. Then, going clockwise around the circle, write every other letter on the blanks.

__ __ __ __ __ __ __ __ __ __ __

**King Trollex is the upbeat leader of the Techno Trolls.
The Techno Trolls are mermaid Trolls.**

Techno Trolls are the world's biggest fans of techno and dubstep.

Where do the Techno Trolls live? To find out, start at the arrow. Then, going clockwise around the circle, write every other letter on the blanks.

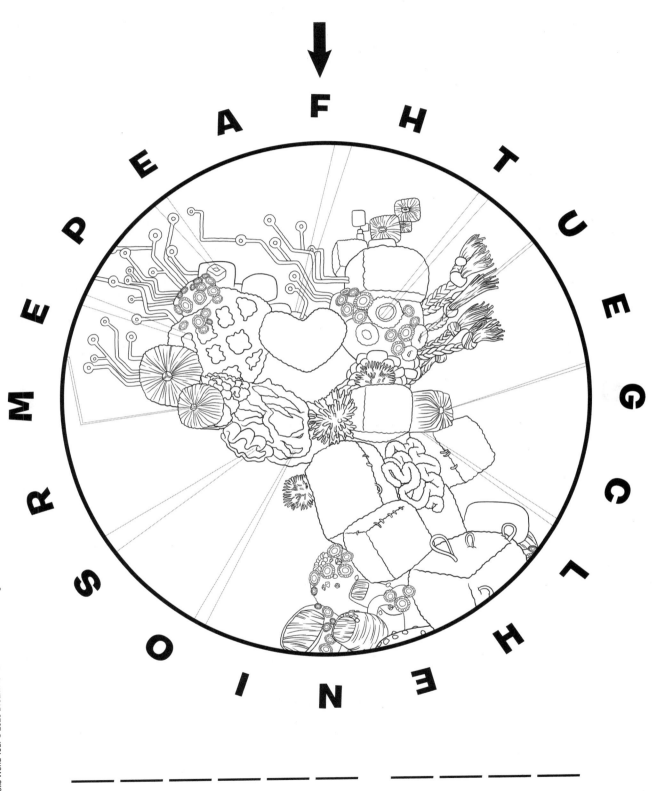

F H T U E G C I H E N I O S R M E P E A

___ ___ ___ ___ ___ ___   ___ ___ ___ ___

ANSWER: Techno Reef.

Poppy and Branch's next stop is to visit the Country Western Trolls. Use the key to find out where they live!

L O N E S O M E   F L A T S

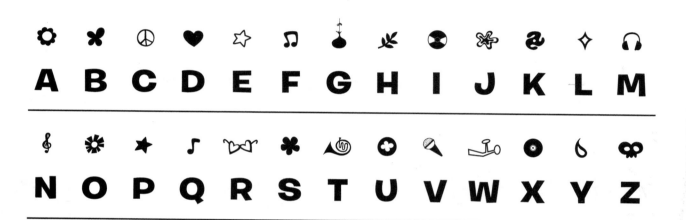

Meet Mayor Delta Dawn! She's the leader of the Country Western Trolls.

This is Hickory! He is a Country Western Troll.

What is Hickory running to? Draw it!

The Rocker Trolls live in Volcano Rock City.
Draw a volcano where they can rock out!

Barb is Queen of the Rocker Trolls!
She wants rock to be the only kind of music.

Barb's pet bat is named Debbie.
Draw your pet, or your favorite animal!

**King Thrash is the retired King of the Rocker Trolls.
He is Barb's dad.**

Riff is a die-hard rocker, and Barb's right-hand man!

This rocker may be small, but she can rock harder and louder than any Troll out there!

Music is life!

What is your favorite song?

_____

_____

Who is your favorite musical artist?

_____

_____

What is your favorite type of music?

_____

_____

Can you play any instruments? If not, do you want to learn to play one?

_____

_____

What is your favorite Trolls World Tour song?

_____

_____

Musical Sudoku

Complete the puzzle by filling in the blanks. Every row, column, and block should include all musical genres.

P = POP • C = COUNTRY WESTERN
S = CLASSICAL • F = FUNK
T = TECHNO • R = ROCK

P		S		C	
	C		F		P
F					R
		T	S	F	
C	R		T		
		P		R	

ANSWER:

P	F	S	R	C	T
T	C	R	F	S	P
F	S	C	P	T	R
R	P	T	S	F	C
C	R	F	T	P	S
S	T	P	C	R	F

Poppy and Branch travel all over Trolls Kingdom!
Where have you traveled to?

I Love YOU

Draw your favorite place.

You can't harmonize alone!

Here comes *treble.*

Who's who in Trolls Kingdom? Use the clues to find the names of the Trolls leaders!

1. Queen of the Pop Trolls
2. King of the Rocker Trolls
3. King of the Techno Trolls
4. King of the Funk Trolls
5. Leader of the Classical Trolls
6. Mayor of the Country Western Trolls
7. Queen of the Funk Trolls
8. King of the Pop Trolls
9. Queen of the Rocker Trolls
10. Newly returned Prince of the Funk Trolls

```
R E P O O C R L S E T S L Z Q E
X T R A C I H G O L E A N D I S
A T Y O H T L A Y C N I U Q N A
E R R S F M R I J D J P O O M B
R O P J T R O L L Z A R T Q D A
I L B C E G L P R T O N W E S R
A L D D C A D S D N O E O U N B
E E E C N E S S E Z T F A R B N
T X J C A S O O L P H R D E F I
Q P A L W D N R T R E N B Y S Y
B O E J E T H R A S H G E P G S
U I R P K L A I D C H O Y P Q I
B C E O Z D F G A S L L O O T P
N P E P P Y U H W I B M N P U K
D X Q L E G D T N S F Z A D L O
```

BRANCH

BRANCH

Reunite the brothers! Help Cooper find Prince D.

START

FINISH

ANSWER:

How many times can you find the word FUNK in the puzzle?

```
C W F D A K N U F
P M U B C T S K L
U J N W R F L Z W
Y T K J Q O U H V
K I A C U H E N I
N C E D S L T R K
U A Y B N P I W R
F D L J H Z A O Y
Y Z C Q F U N K L
```

ANSWER: 5.

Pennywhistle is a happy instrument!

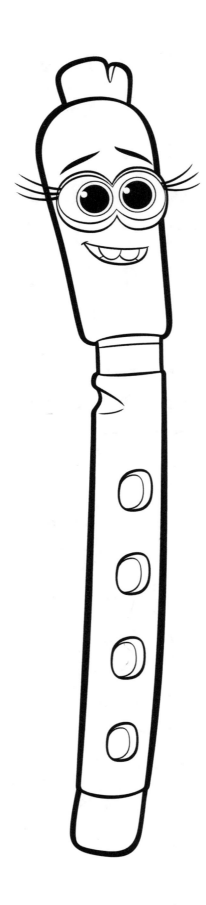

What makes you happy? Draw it here!

What song is Branch dancing to?

_____

Barb wants to go to Vibe City. Help her find the way!

FINISH

START

ANSWER:

Match the Trolls to their names!

1

A
King Peppy

2

B
Biggie

3

C
Queen Barb

4

D
King Quincy

ANSWER: 1-D; 2-C; 3-B; and 4-A.

5

E
Prince D

Prince D

6

F
Trollzart

Trollzart

7

G
King Thrash

King Thrash

8

H
Riff

Riff

ANSWER: 5-H; 6-G; 7-E; and 8-F.

Biggie and Mr. Dinkles want to go on a trip!
Use the key to figure out where they're going.

S Y M P H O N Y V I L L E

**Poppy and Branch travel through Trolls Kingdom
on a flower-faced balloon named Sheila B.!
Draw your favorite way to travel.**

Imagine YOU are a musical Troll!
What's the name of your first album? Draw the cover here!

Rock with Riff!

What song is this Techno Troll dancing to?

Prince D is happy that the royal family is reunited!

Where is Branch going? Draw it!

Feel it!

What instrument is Chaz leaning on? To find out, replace each letter with the one that comes before it in the alphabet. Write the letters on the blanks.

D M B S J O F U

D M B S J O E U

Which picture of Branch matches the one at the top left?

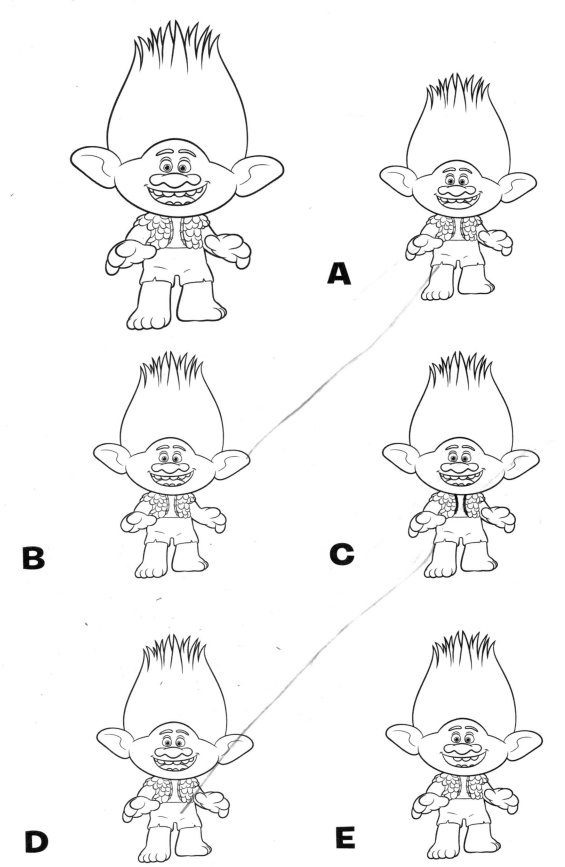

ANSWER: D.

Draw your favorite Pop Troll!

Draw your favorite Rocker Troll!

How many times can you find the word POPPY in the puzzle?

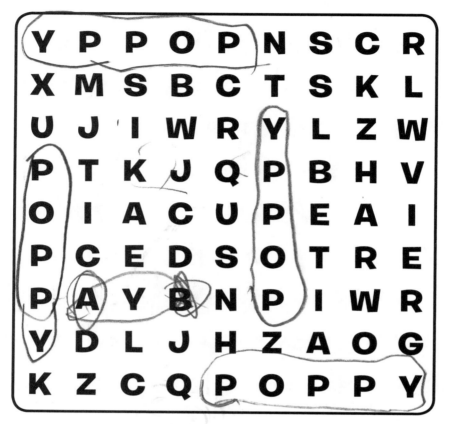

```
Y P P O P N S C R
X M S B C T S K L
U J I W R Y L Z W
P T K J Q P B H V
O I A C U P E A I
P C E D S O T R E
P A Y B N P I W R
Y D L J H Z A O G
K Z C Q P O P P Y
```

Pour some glitter on me!

Draw your favorite Classical Troll!

Draw your favorite Country Western Troll!

Tunks and caicas

Rock your best beat.

Draw your favorite Techno Troll!

Draw your favorite Funk Troll!

Use the key to figure out what Pennywhistle is saying!

Give King Trollex a new hairdo!

Hickory usually wears a hat. Draw his hair!

Who's who? Answer with either King Quincy or Delta Dawn.

1. Who is a mayor?

_____

2. Who has a long-lost son?

_____

3. Who has a gold cape?

_____

4. Who plays sadder songs (according to Poppy)?

_____

5. Who has a flying city?

_____

ANSWER: 1. Delta Dawn; 2. King Quincy; 3. King Quincy; 4. Delta Dawn; and 5. King Quincy.

Write a song for Poppy and Barb to sing together!

_____

_____

_____

_____

_____

_____

_____

_____

_____

_____

_____

_____

_____

_____

_____

_____

_____

_____

_____

_____

_____

_____

_____

_____

_____

_____

_____

_____

_____

_____

_____

_____

_____

_____

_____

_____

Match each citizen to their town!

1

A
Symphonyville

2

B
Volcano Rock City

3

C
Vibe City

4

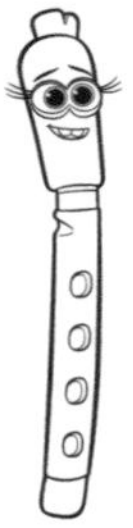

D
Trolls Village

5

E
Lonesome Flats

Draw YOURSELF dancing with Poppy!

Learn to draw a Troll!

Help Poppy get back home to King Peppy!

START

FINISH

Trisha

ANSWER:

Funky hair, don't care!

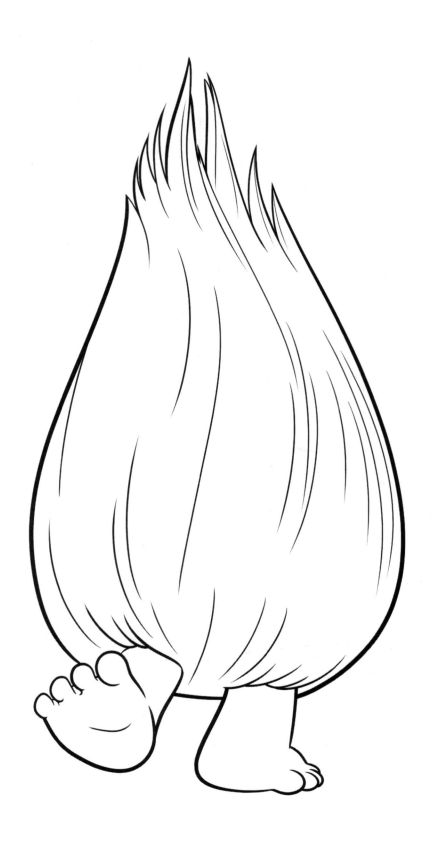

What is Branch saying?

POWER of the STRINGS

Barb and the Rocker Trolls!

If you and your friends formed a band, what would the name be? Draw yourselves in your band!

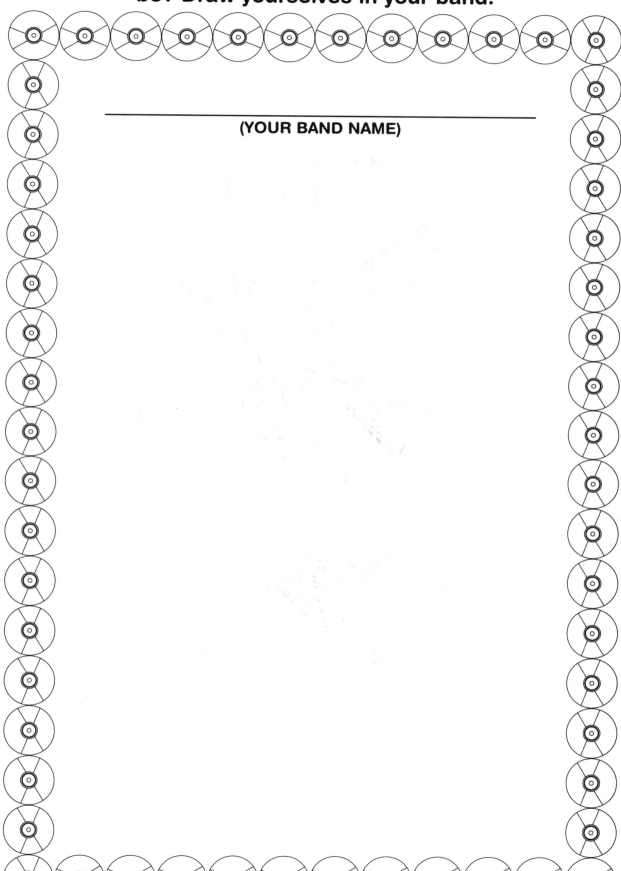

_____

(YOUR BAND NAME)

Give Tiny Diamond some BIG hair!

Branch needs cheering up.
Which path will lead Poppy to Branch?

A

B

C

Be free!

Can you match these Trolls with their shadows?

ANSWER: 1-D; 2-C; 3-B; and 4-A.

Gonna have to dance for it!

Living that Poppy life!

Troll Dots!

(For two players)

With a friend, take turns drawing a line to connect two dots. If you complete a box, write your initials in it and take another turn. Each player gets one point for a regular box and two points for a Troll box. At the end of the game, the player with more points wins!

More Troll dots!

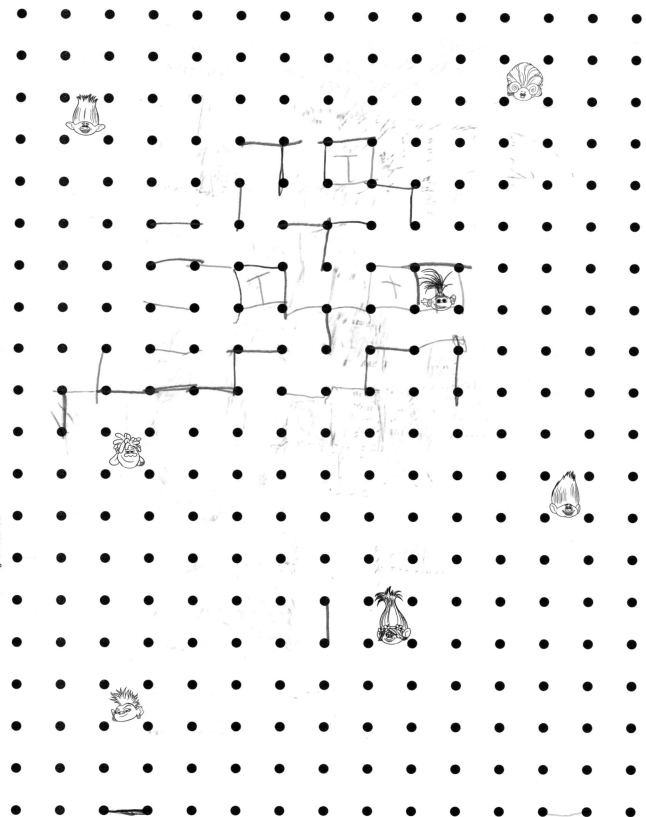

Hug Time!

Use the key to find out what Hickory is saying to Poppy.

"You may be __P__ __O__ __P__, and I may be

__C__ __O__ __U__ __N__ __T__ __R__ __Y__, but Trolls

are __T__ __R__ __O__ __L__ __L__ __S__."

✿	✖	☮	♥	☆	♫	🎸	🍃	◉	✳	@	◇	🎧
A	**B**	**C**	**D**	**E**	**F**	**G**	**H**	**I**	**J**	**K**	**L**	**M**

🎼	❋	★	♪	〰	✤	📯	⊕	🎤	⚓	⊙	◗	☠
N	**O**	**P**	**Q**	**R**	**S**	**T**	**U**	**V**	**W**	**X**	**Y**	**Z**

The Country Western Trolls live in Lonesome Flats.
Draw where you live!

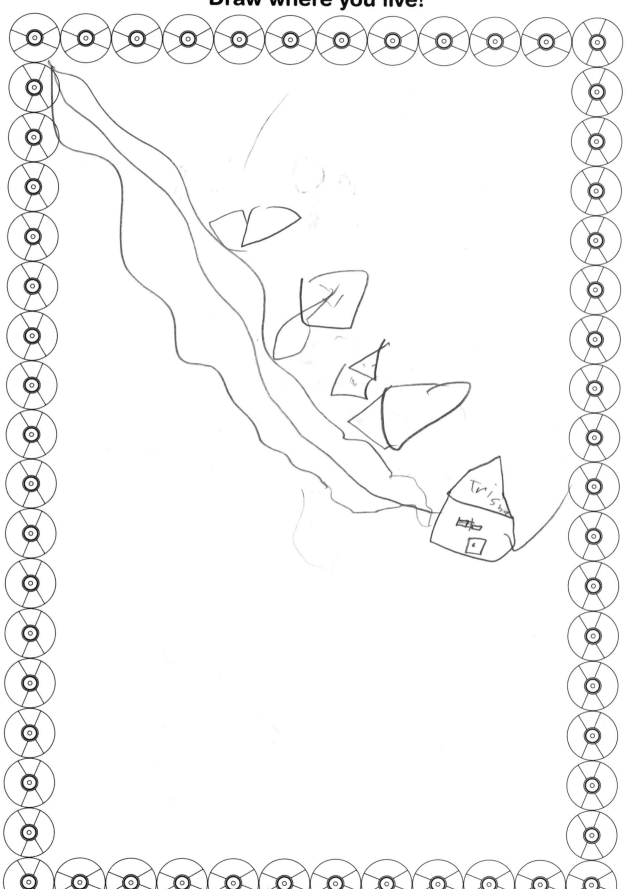

Troll-a-tronic!

Troll-a-delic!

All the jams!

Help Branch find his way through the maze to get to Poppy!

FINISH

START

ANSWER:

In need of a high five!

Who is this? To find out, replace each letter with the one that comes after it in the alphabet.

B K N T C F T X

c l m v d g u y

ANSWER: Cloud Guy.

This is Smidge. She is a Pop Troll with a deep baritone voice.

Circle the picture of Smidge that matches the one at the top left.

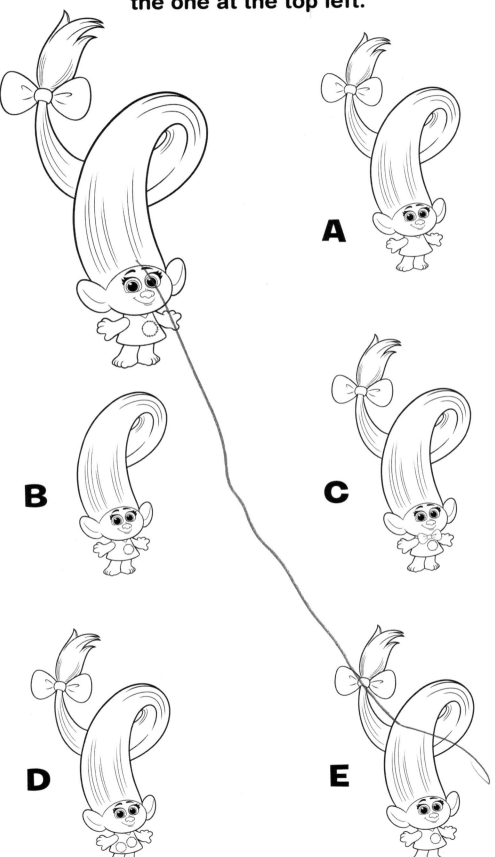

A

B

C

D

E

ANSWER: E.

I love rock!

I love pop!

Drop that beat!

How many times can you find the word MUSIC in the puzzle?

```
C W M U S I C F C
P A I B C T S K L
U J F W R P L Z W
D T S J Q I Y H V
T I A C I S U M C
A C E D S L T R I
I A Y B N P C W S
M U S I C Z A O U
Y Z C Q A R E I M
```

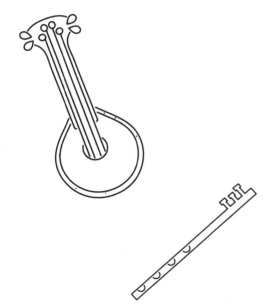

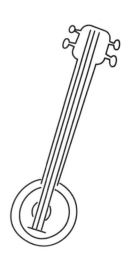

ANSWER: 4.

```
C W M U S I C F C
P A I B C T S K L
U J F W R P L Z W
D T S J Q I Y H V
T I A C I S U M C
A C E D S L T R I
I A Y B N P C W S
M U S I C Z A O U
Y Z C Q A R E I M
```

Match the Trolls to their musical genre.

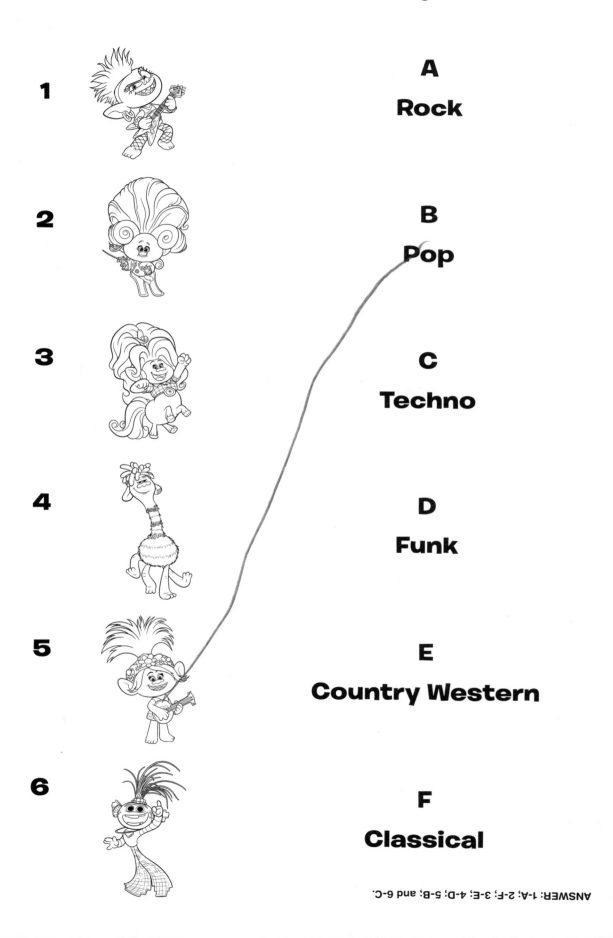

1

2

3

4

5

6

A

Rock

B

Pop

C

Techno

D

Funk

E

Country Western

F

Classical

Trolls memory game!

How much do you remember about the picture on the previous page?

1. What kind of music do the Trolls play?

_____

2. What is on Barb's guitar?

_____

3. What is the Troll on the bottom right holding?

_____

4. Which Troll is wearing a hat?

_____

5. How many total earrings do you see on the Trolls?

_____

What do you think Poppy and Barb are saying?

Life is full of music.
How many musical notes can you count?

Draw Branch rockin' a rainbow hairstyle!

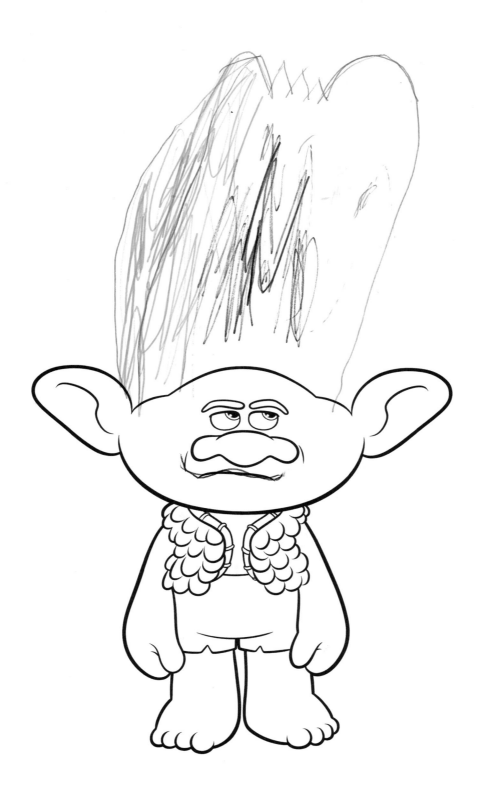

Fill in the missing letters to spell the names of these Trolls:

1. NOPP_Q

2. BR SIVH

3. C_OP QR

4. G_HI D EEMOND

5. T YVV DI JKLND

6. QAR Q

7. HI _____RY

8. D_Q_QTA D_Q_QN

9. _ENNY _HISTLE

10. K L_QG TR S JYEX

Draw yourself as a Troll!

Perfect harmony!